Izzie: Book Three
PATRICIA'S
SECRET
BUDGE WILSON

Izzie: Book Three
PATRICIA'S SECRET

BUDGE WILSON

PENGUIN
CANADA

PENGUIN CANADA

Published by the Penguin Group

Penguin Group (Canada), 90 Eglinton Avenue East, Suite 700, Toronto, Ontario, Canada M4P 2Y3
(a division of Pearson Penguin Canada Inc.)

Penguin Group (USA) Inc., 375 Hudson Street, New York, New York 10014, U.S.A.
Penguin Books Ltd, 80 Strand, London WC2R 0RL, England
Penguin Ireland, 25 St Stephen's Green, Dublin 2, Ireland (a division of Penguin Books Ltd)
Penguin Group (Australia), 250 Camberwell Road, Camberwell, Victoria 3124, Australia
(a division of Pearson Australia Group Pty Ltd)
Penguin Books India Pvt Ltd, 11 Community Centre, Panchsheel Park, New Delhi – 110 017, India
Penguin Group (NZ), cnr Airborne and Rosedale Roads, Albany, Auckland 1310, New Zealand
(a division of Pearson New Zealand Ltd)
Penguin Books (South Africa) (Pty) Ltd, 24 Sturdee Avenue, Rosebank, Johannesburg 2196,
South Africa

Penguin Books Ltd, Registered Offices: 80 Strand, London WC2R 0RL, England

First published 2005

1 2 3 4 5 6 7 8 9 10   (WEB)

Manufactured in Canada.

LIBRARY AND ARCHIVES CANADA CATALOGUING IN PUBLICATION

Wilson, Budge
Izzie : Patricia's secret / Budge Wilson.

(Our Canadian girl)
"Izzie: book three".
ISBN 0-14-305007-9

I. Title. II. Title: Patricia's secret. III. Series.

PS8595.I5813I987   2005   jC813'.54   C2005-902903-X

Visit the Penguin Group (Canada) website at **www.penguin.ca**

This book is for
my long-time friend
Helga Knop

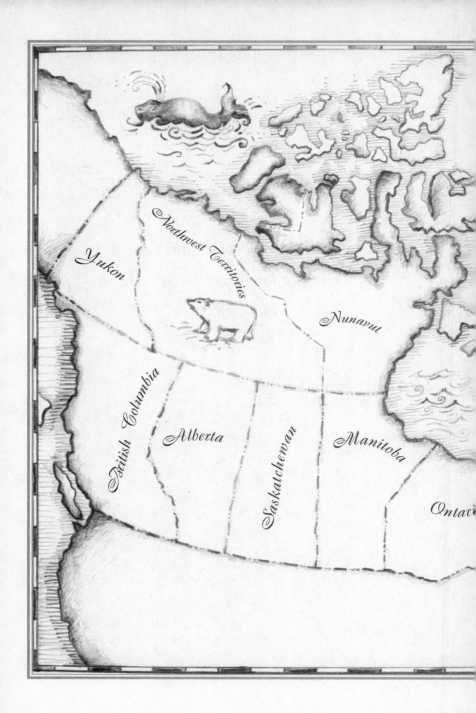

Canada

Quebec

Newfoundland and Labrador

New Brunswick

P.E.I.

Nova Scotia

 Marks the location of the story

IZZIE'S STORY CONTINUES

E VER SINCE THEY HAD TO LEAVE the peaceful village of Granite Cove, Nova Scotia, Izzie, her mother, and her brother, Joey, have been living a new kind of life in Woodside, on the outskirts of Dartmouth. Mrs. Publicover has a job on the assembly line at the sugar refinery, and Izzie and Joey have found new friends. From the hill across the road, they have a wide view of Halifax Harbour and McNab's Island.

It's June 1942 now. The progress of the war in Europe is still very uncertain, and it's a cause for great concern. There is also much violence and destruction on the stormy waters of the North Atlantic. Izzie's father is in the navy—on a corvette—and he's out there somewhere on that cold and dangerous sea. It's impossible for the family not to worry about him when they see explosions in the night, just beyond Halifax Harbour, or when they hear news of the sinking of another ship.

The other hardships of war are still with them: food and fuel rationing, the scarcity of many materials, blackout restrictions, grim news from friends and neighbours fighting overseas. But for Izzie and Joey, nothing can compare with the fear they feel for the safety of their own father. They're afraid they may open the newspaper one day and find his name among the lists of men and women who have died or been wounded.

However, life is also exciting in wartime Dartmouth and Halifax. Izzie can't help but enjoy the luminous dance of the searchlights at night, the uneasy thrill she feels at the sound of the air-raid sirens, the silence of the huge ships as they move in and out of the harbour in their convoys. The searchlights and sirens are just practising, but the convoys are for real.

One day, Izzie says to her mother, "I feel like I'm balanced on the edge of something." When her mother asks what she means, Izzie can't explain. She isn't even sure she understands the feeling herself. But she does know that an edge has two sides to it. And she's aware that in spite of the fears they are all feeling, the family is finding much to enjoy about their life in Woodside. So there are pleasurable things on one side of the edge and very difficult things on the other. This combination can sometimes make Izzie feel very confused.

CHAPTER N° 1

When Izzie woke up early, she always did a lot of thinking before she got out of bed. This morning she opened her eyes when it was still dark, and she lay there staring at the ceiling—remembering how, just a few weeks ago, the flames from the burning *Trongate* had bathed the whole room with a flickering red glow. She recalled how close that munitions ship had come to blowing up much of Dartmouth and Halifax. And yet, the chilling sounds of the air-raid siren drills excited her, as did the harbour full of vessels from all over the world. Izzie also realized that she had come to enjoy living so close to a big city—a big *wartime* city. Ashamed though she was to admit it, she almost enjoyed the war. But it was a big *almost*. After all, her father was a part of that war, and he was sailing across an ocean that was full of U-boats—or submarines—that were carrying deadly torpedoes.

Izzie could hear Rosalie and her mother talking in the kitchen. But still she didn't move. She was thinking back to her carefree days in Granite Cove, where her father had been a fisherman, when life had seemed so simple. No electricity or running water, milk that came out of a cow instead of a bottle, a lot of water to carry and logs to split, but yes, simple. Izzie sighed. It had been sad to leave the place that she loved so much, and it had been especially hard to say goodbye to her best friend, Jasper.

But things were OK here, too. Very OK, in fact. For the first time in her life, Izzie had two best friends who were girls—Roberta, who was so quiet and shy, and who never acted mad or mean, and Patricia, who was one of the many British guest children who had been sent to Canada to protect them from the Nazi bombs. There were things about Izzie and Patricia that differed from the other kids in their school: their unfamiliar accents, their clothes, their way of going about their lives—Patricia, withdrawn and stiff, Izzie, outspoken and impulsive. Being different from the others had created an odd sort of bond between them. Otherwise, they probably wouldn't have been drawn to each other.

And Rosalie! They were living in Rosalie's house, and for Izzie it was like having two mothers. First of all, there was her own sweet, loving mother, who worried a lot. Then there was Rosalie, who seemed to be dancing through life, with her red blouses, high heels, dangling earrings, and swarms of boyfriends.

Izzie smiled quietly to herself. She added it all up: the wartime excitement of a big city, new friends, new things to see and do. Yes, this was a good place to live.

But all of this thinking was taking up a lot of time. Izzie could hear the clattering of dishes and voices rising up from the kitchen. Finally, she decided she'd have to leave her warm bed if she didn't want to be late for school.

CHAPTER №. 2

When Izzie's cat, Adella, came upstairs to see what was keeping her, Izzie knew it really was time to get up. But as she was putting on her clothes, she was still thinking about her new Woodside friends. It was easy to see why she liked Roberta. After all, Roberta was always calm and cheerful, and she also liked Izzie a lot. *That's* always a plus. Izzie wondered if Roberta liked her because Izzie wasn't afraid to take risks, get angry out loud, and stand up for herself. Maybe Izzie was a sort of heroine for Roberta—the kind of person that Roberta would have liked to be herself.

But Patricia? Why on earth had Patricia become Izzie's friend? She was moody and secretive and did a lot of complaining about Canadian weather, Canadian accents, and Canadian manners. And she did quite a bit of bragging about her brave mother and important father—who was a commander in the British navy, for heaven's sake! She also talked on and on about the marvels and perfections of England. Boring! But Izzie had the feeling that Patricia was still keeping a lot of heavy secrets inside her. After the *Trongate* fire, Patricia had finally been able to loosen up a bit, but then she'd started to retreat back into her old self. Maybe Izzie put up with Patricia because she was like a puzzle that Izzie was dying to solve. And Patricia seemed to *need* Izzie's friendship in a peculiar sort of way. Izzie had to admit to herself that it was nice to feel needed.

Suddenly, Izzie heard Joey clattering up the stairs, yelling her name. Usually, he kept pretty much to himself, but right now, he was sounding kind of frantic.

Izzie opened her bedroom door as he flew into her room.

"Bad news!" he was yelling. "Disaster! I can't stand it!" Then he started to cry.

Izzie piled a couple of blankets on top of the heat register so that no one downstairs would hear the racket. Joey was a lot younger than she was, so she felt she had to get him to simmer down before he boiled right over. She put her hands on his shoulders and said, in a voice remarkably like her mother's, "What is it? Tell me what's wrong. Then maybe you'll feel better about it."

Instead, Joey's mouth screwed up and his tears spilled over again. "I don't even know who I am any more," he wailed, "or where I'm supposed to be. I want it to be like it used to be."

Izzie could feel her motherly-big-sister act faltering. In fact, she was feeling pretty impatient. She took her hands off Joey's shoulders and said, "Well, *tell* me! I can't help you if you don't *tell* me anything!"

Joey hiccupped into silence and took a deep breath. "I heard Rosalie and Mum talking in the kitchen. You're not the only one who listens to the grown-ups when they don't know you can hear."

"OK! *OK!* What did you hear?" Izzie suddenly thought it might be something awful about their father. *"Hurry!"*

"They said the sugar refinery is going to close. Mum and Rosalie will lose their jobs. We won't be able to live in this nice house with Rosalie any more. And we can't go back and live in Granite Cove. The *Eisners* live in our old house. And Dad's away, so he can't fix things and make everything right." Joey was an extremely wet crier. His face looked as though it had sprung a very big leak.

Uh-oh, thought Izzie. *Joey's right. This is a disaster.* Out loud she said, "C'mon. Let's get downstairs fast and find out exactly what's going on."

*"I don't even know who I
am any more," he wailed,
"or where I'm supposed
to be. I want it to be
like it used to be."*

CHAPTER N° 3

It was all true. Even though the kids might be late for school and Rosalie and Mrs. Publicover might be late for work, they all sat down around the kitchen table and talked about the awful news.

Yes, the sugar refinery was closing.

"But, gee whiz," insisted Izzie, "surely people still need sugar."

"Yes," said her mother, "but the navy needs a ship-refitting centre even more—a place to fix up damaged vessels and make them fit to sail again. The refinery building is a perfect place for it—right on the harbour and all, with a good

11

wharf and deep water." She looked at Izzie and Joey and sighed. "There happens to be a war on," she added with a thin smile.

Rosalie's smile was a little more convincing. "It's not the end of the world, you know," she said. "So don't have a big conniption fit." She was buttering their toast and reaching for the peanut butter. "Your mum and I will probably be able to get new jobs pretty quickly, and, well … we'll all find somewhere else to live."

Somewhere else! Izzie suddenly realized how much she liked living exactly where she was.

That night, Izzie wrote a letter to her father.

Dear Dad,

Now we have to move again. And maybe Mum won't be able to get another job fast enough. How will we be able to send money to Grandma and Grandpa? And I like it here. I like living right on the harbour and seeing the big boats sailing by. I hate moving all the time. Maybe I'll never see Roberta and Patricia again. Roberta's dad almost runs the sugar refinery, and the Johnstones work there too. That's the family Patricia lives with. Maybe I'll never, never discover what makes Patricia tick.

I'm sorry for you out there on the cold and dangerous sea, but I hope it's OK for me to say that I'm feeling sorry for me, too, tonight. Just like Joey, I feel like I don't belong anywhere any more.

My next letter will be more cheerful. I promise. But I needed to get that out before I busted wide open. And you wouldn't like that, would you?

> *Your loving daughter,*
> *Izzie*

CHAPTER N°4

The next day, Izzie and Joey walked home from school together. Usually, Izzie enjoyed the walk, with the harbour on their right, where something was always going on. But today there was no bounce in her step. She'd had a terrible day, thinking and thinking about having to move.

Telling her friends had been even worse. When she'd given the news to Roberta, Roberta hadn't said a single thing. She'd just gone off to the girls' washroom, with her shoulders hunched over. Then she'd sat in one of the cubicles and cried. Izzie could hear her.

When she'd told Patricia, Patricia had looked more angry than sad. "That means the Johnstones will have to leave too. I could find myself living in Vancouver, and you could end up at the North Pole. We've just been set afloat like a lot of flotsam and jetsam on the surface of the sea." Then she frowned extra hard. "It occurs to me," she said, in her thickest English accent, "that I've been afloat for my entire life."

However, by the time Izzie and Joey returned from school, Rosalie had managed to put a whole new spin on everything. It amazed Izzie that so much could happen in so little time. When they walked in the front door, they could see Rosalie standing in the entrance to the kitchen with a big smile on her face. The sun was shining on her red blouse, and something heavy on Izzie's shoulders lifted right off.

"Everything's going to be *fine!*" said Rosalie. She started to talk so fast—and for so long—that Izzie grabbed a stool from the living room and sat down on it. The load of misery she'd been carrying around all day had made her feel very tired. But here, after all that, was Rosalie, talking very quickly.

"I've found out," she said, "that we'll all be allowed to stay in our houses. I've also been offered a job in September in the new ship-refitting centre, doing the books, like I'm doing at the sugar refinery right now. So that looks after *me*. And also you kids, because we can all still live here. I heard this afternoon that Roberta's father will have a fancy new job overseeing some of the staff at the new place, instead of helping to run the sugar refinery, so they get to keep their same big executive house. Therefore …," and she paused as though preparing for the closing lines in a big speech, *"we'll still all be together."*

Izzie was sitting up on the stool, straighter and straighter. She should have known that Rosalie would be able to push that weight right off her back and shoulders. But she didn't get off the stool or say anything. She didn't want to miss a single word of what Rosalie was saying.

"So that left your mum dangling on a string— no job and those grandparents in Granite Cove waiting for their monthly cheque to arrive from her." She paused here, looking at their mother, who had emerged from the kitchen to join the group. Mrs. Publicover was standing there, looking so calm and serene and almost … *smug!*

But Rosalie picked up steam again. "So I drove her up to Imperial Oil, to the oil refinery there. Yes, they'll need a new secretary by September 15. If your mum can learn to type fast enough by then, they'll hire her. She answered all the manager's questions beautifully, and—what's even better—I could see that he liked her a lot. She was also looking especially pretty. I made her put on a tiny bit of my makeup, and she wore that navy blue suit of mine that I never wear, over that frilly white blouse that she keeps for when your father's on leave. And guess what! The manager's great-great-grandfather was a Publicover and lived in a fishing village. Before we left, they were joking about being first cousins."

Then Rosalie moved away from the kitchen door and pointed inside. Izzie jumped up, and she and Joey rushed over to look. There, on the kitchen table, beside the dishes laid out for supper, was a typewriter. It was huge, and its keys were black with metal rims and white letters. There was already a sheet of paper in it, and it said, "My name is Bessie Publicover. My children are Izzie and Joey. My husband is a brave sailor. Rosalie is my best friend. I have a new job." Mrs. Publicover was grinning. "It took me a whole hour to type that!" she said.

Rosalie grinned. "The manager—Mr. Simmons—lent the typewriter to her so she could learn how to use it at home. I really think he has kind of a crush on your mother."

Izzie and Joey laughed. People didn't have crushes on your parents! Or did they?

They looked hard at their mother, with her naturally curly auburn hair (but not bright orange and frizzy like Izzie's), her perfect pale skin, and her quiet smile. Yes. She was only a mother, but they could see that she was certainly someone a person could have a crush on.

Izzie woke up very early the next morning, even though it was Saturday. Why? But she soon knew the answer to that question. She could hear a loud *clack, clack, clack* from the kitchen. It was a SLOW *clack, clack, clack,* but it was very firm. Her mother must be practising on her new typewriter. Izzie rushed downstairs to check out the scene. There her mother was—not even out of her nightie yet—pecking away at the keys with her two index fingers. But she was smiling as she pecked.

When she saw Izzie, she laughed. "Sorry to wake

you up," she said. "But I have so much to learn in so few weeks that I can't waste a single minute."

Izzie grinned. "Is it hard?" she asked.

"Yes," said her mum. "Very. First, I have to learn where all the numbers and letters are and other stuff, like periods and semicolons. And to remember to leave spaces. Then, I have to learn how to do it with all my fingers. *Then,*" her mother's eyes opened very wide, "I have to learn how to do it without looking at the keys! That's a lot to learn in three months."

"But you're smiling so hard," said Izzie.

Her mother laughed. "That's because it's such fun!" she said. "I haven't had this much fun since I learned how to do my first jigsaw puzzle." Then she looked very serious. "But fun or not, I just hope I can learn all that by the time September 15 rolls around. Fun? *Yes.* Easy? *No.* I'm not even sure how to go about learning what to do and how to do it."

Right at that point in the conversation, Rosalie came clicking into the kitchen in her high heels.

She was carrying a book, a roll of white adhesive tape, and a pair of scissors. She also had a big smile on her face.

"Nothing to worry about!" she announced, sitting down at the kitchen table and starting to peel off the tape and cut it into small circles. She stuck the white disks all up and down her arm as she cut them out. Puzzled, everyone was silent, watching her.

"I have a book here," she said, as she stuck piece after piece on her arm, "called *How to Become a Typist in Twenty-Five Easy Lessons*. It's one of my old books from when I was at the Maritime Business College. It made a crack typist out of me, and it wasn't hard. So forget all that *'not easy'* stuff. You just have to do exactly what the book says."

"Like what?" asked Izzie. "Why does she need a book? Why can't she just practise?"

"You'll see." Rosalie smiled and got up from her chair to stand behind Mrs. Publicover. Then, to their horror, Rosalie started peeling off the little white disks and placing one on top of each typewriter key. She pressed each one hard, to make sure it was stuck on *tight*.

Mrs. Publicover looked almost as though she might cry. "Why on earth did you do *that*? Now I can't see what letters I'm hitting." She reached out to peel off one of the circles. Izzie moved forward to help her.

Rosalie pulled Mrs. Publicover's hand away from the key. With her other arm, she made a barrier to keep Izzie away from the typewriter.

"The book will tell you what to do next, but I'll give you a little preview. First, you learn what the letters are on the middle row of keys. There's a chart in the book that will show you. And you learn which finger to put on which key. Not just your index finger. *All* your fingers—and thumbs for spacing."

"Only one row?" asked Joey. "Why?" He'd been watching from the doorway.

"Because you learn better if you memorize things in small pieces."

"Hmm!" said Izzie. She was thinking about the long poem she had to learn by heart for school. She'd been trying to learn the whole poem in one gulp, and it wasn't working. Maybe if she took one line at a time until she had each one completely chewed, swallowed, and digested ...

But Rosalie was still talking. "After you learn the letters of that row—and the fingering—the book will give you little exercises to do."

"Like what?" said Izzie.

"Like asking you to type *a* or *l* or *s* or *h*. Soon you can do it without even thinking."

"And then?" Mrs. Publicover was looking more hopeful. "Can we peel off the tape?"

"No!" said Rosalie. "So don't let me catch you peeking under it! Then you get to type words with the middle row. Like *ash* or *sad* or *dash* or *lad*. And when you graduate to the next row, even tiny little sentences."

Mrs. Publicover sighed. "But not enough to write a whole letter to your husband. I was planning to write Jeff a letter that would amaze

"After you learn the letters of that row—and the fingering— the book will give you little exercises to do."

him so much that he'd fall right off the deck of his vessel!"

Rosalie laughed. "Once you get through that big performance with all three rows of letters, that's exactly what you'll be able to do." Then she calmed down and was serious. "Honest, Bessie. You won't believe how fast you'll learn. Just wait'll you start tapping those blank keys and begin to see real words come up on the paper. If you think it's fun *now*, just see how you feel when *that* happens. It's like a small miracle. You'll be thrilled right out of your skin!"

Everyone was looking hard at Mrs. Publicover. At last, she gave them all a big smile and reached out her hand. "Give me that book," she said. "And everyone scram out of the kitchen and leave me in peace. I have a lot of work to do."

CHAPTER Nº 6

Later that day, Izzie cut open the letter that she'd written to her father the day before. She hadn't known whether she should send a complaining letter to someone who might be torpedoed five minutes after he got the letter, so she hadn't mailed it yet. She decided now that she'd keep the miserable letter in the envelope but add a new one. Leaving the sad one in would make the second one … what? She searched around in her head for the word she wanted. Then she knew. It would make the second one more *dramatic*.

Dear Dad,

It was only two days ago that I wrote that other letter. But look at all the things that have happened since then! We get to stay in Rosalie's house. She has a new job with the ship-refitting place. Roberta and Patricia will still be here, too.

But the big thing is this. Mum has a new job at the oil refinery in September. The boss likes her. She wore some of Rosalie's makeup. Also, his great-great-grandfather was a Publicover in a fishing village. I don't know if it was the lipstick or the grandfather that got her the job.

Mum has to learn to type. Her new boss lent her a typewriter, and Rosalie gave her a book that teaches how to do it. Rosalie put white tape on all the keys. Poor Mum. Now she can't see the letters. But she's very brave and also very <u>determined</u>. I was going to say <u>stubborn</u>, but I looked it up in my school dictionary, and I decided that <u>determined</u> was a nicer word.

I'm going to read Mum's book when she's not around and maybe even try typing on her blank typewriter. Then I can become a secretary if you need someone to support you in your old age.

Love,

Izzie

On the following day, Izzie wrote a letter to Jasper, her best friend in Granite Cove.

Dear Jasper,

Three days ago, I thought the world had come to an end. Mum lost her job. We were going to have to move again. Rosalie and Roberta and Patricia would all be gone from my life. We wouldn't have had any money to send to Grandma and Grandpa. And nowhere to live.

Today everything is perfect—or almost. We need to have Dad come home safe and sound for it to be perfect. And for you to come and live in Woodside.

But Mum has a job. We don't have to move. Rosalie will still be here to make us all happy. Wait till you meet her. She's like a fairy godmother to the whole family. You can't believe the wild earrings she wears. Or how high her heels are.

A big piece of me is still homesick for Granite Cove. But Mum says that in this life we can't expect to have everything. What other life does she have in mind?

Your best friend,
Izzie

That evening Izzie added a P.S. to Jasper's letter.

P.S. Hey! Listen to this! It looks as if we can expect to have nearly everything!

Guess what? You probably know what, already. We got a letter today from Mr. Eisner. In July, they have to go to Canso for a couple of months to look after his sick mother. He asked if Mum had any vacation from her job. Vacation! Yeah. Like no job till September. He asked if we could find anyone to come and live in our house in Granite Cove for two months, in case she couldn't leave her job for that long. They need someone to look after the shop and the cows and the stupid chickens.

Can you believe all that? So we're going home! There's still a war on, with bad things happening, and Dad's out there on a sea that's full of dangerous submarines. But the rest is good.

And that's not all. Rosalie is coming with us for her own long holiday. And the Johnstones, the people Patricia lives with, want to visit their family in Winnipeg. So we asked Patricia to come and spend the summer in Granite Cove. Roberta's going to Cow Bay with her parents, so Patricia would lose all her friends for two whole months.

Don't be jealous of my friendship with Patricia. She's so peculiar that there's nothing to make you jealous. She's certainly my friend, but I'm not sure how I feel about spending a _whole summer_ with her—in the same bedroom, even. We may be scratching each other's eyes out by the end of August. She's always busy being so _British_ and so _high class_ that if she starts acting snobby *about Granite Cove, I may push her off the Government Wharf.*

What a long letter! You have time for one letter to me before we arrive in Granite Cove. So—do it!

Izzie

Two weeks later, the same truck that had carried a weeping Izzie out of Granite Cove in January brought her back home in July. The truck jiggled over the ruts in the road, with Mrs. Publicover driving, Rosalie and Joey in the front seat, Izzie and Patricia crammed into the open cab with all their boxes and suitcases—and Adella in her cat basket.

"There's no running water, you know." said Izzie, when they were about twenty minutes from Granite Cove. "We carry it from the well in buckets." She looked at Patricia, but she couldn't tell what Patricia was thinking.

"And we don't have electricity. So we have to light our lamps with matches. And clean the yucky chimneys."

Patricia still didn't say anything. Izzie tried something more cheerful.

"Jasper will be there. He's my very best friend in Granite Cove. You'll like him a lot." Patricia frowned and still said nothing. *Jealous,* thought Izzie, *before she even meets him.*

"And you'll like the telephone," said Izzie. "We have a party line. That means that if Mum is out, we can listen to other people's conversations. Sometimes you hear amazing secrets. But don't tell that to *anyone.* It's *strictly forbidden* in our family to do that. But of course everyone does it. So if you hate living with the Publicovers, don't tell that to anyone on the phone. It would be like putting that information on a big sign and nailing it to one of the big posts on the Government Wharf."

Patricia looked at Izzie and grinned. "I expect that will be a heap of fun," she said. "A jolly good idea." She sounded even more British than usual. It made Izzie realize that Patricia must have been trying really hard to speak like a Canadian. But for a moment, she'd forgotten. The thought of a phone with a party line must have driven all that carefulness right out of her head.

Well! thought Izzie. *At least I struck oil on that one.*

On the following afternoon, Izzie wrote a long letter to her father.

Dear Dad,

We're back home. I wish you were with us, to make it all perfect. It feels so good to be here that I don't even miss the electric lights or the toilet that flushes or Rosalie's little red radio. She brought it with her, because she forgot about there being no way to plug it in!

I worried a bit that Rosalie's wild clothes and heavy lipstick and stuff might make some of the women mad. Sometimes women can be funny about things like that. I'm not a woman yet, but I do a lot of watching. I've noticed that wives like other women to look as invisible as possible, so that their husbands won't get too enchanted by them.

But maybe Rosalie knows all that without being told. Anyway, she arrived in Granite Cove wearing a pair of navy blue slacks (that's like women's trousers) and a light blue sweater. And sneakers! No high heels. She did have on a pair of pretty crazy earrings, but I guess the Cove ladies will forgive her for that. I mentioned her clothes to Mum when we went to the well for water, and she said that she figured Rosalie was "testing the waters." Pretty smart of Rosalie, eh?

Patricia is jealous of my friendship with Jasper, and he's jealous of her. You can tell that already, and we've only been here for a day. It seems like they don't even know how to <u>smile</u> at each other. Oh, well.

Clementine and I had a lovely reunion. Cows are such soothing animals. It made me feel so good to have her warm body against mine. If I grow up and marry a city man, I'm going to have to bring a cow with me, even if we live in an apartment building. It could be pretty tricky going up and down in the elevator, but I'd sure like to give it a try.

Adella knew we were home and jumped right up on the kitchen couch where she always liked to sleep. She lay there with her eyes half closed. You could tell she loved being back. Cats are smarter than most people think.

Three of the Cove ladies brought us over baked beans and brown bread for supper. And a lot of chocolate brownies and coconut squares. I bet they used up most of their sugar ration for July. And Mr. Henkel gave us a great big bag of cod tongues and cheeks. Also two big mackerel. Mrs. Jollimore came over with lettuce from her garden.

Patricia isn't saying anything bad about the oil lamps or the outhouse or how heavy the water buckets are. She just looks and looks at everything, like she never saw anything like Granite Cove before. And I bet she never did. I told her that she doesn't have to eat the cod tongues and cheeks. She cranked up a lukewarm smile and said, "Good."

I want you to be here with us. Don't let anything bad happen to you.

Love,

Izzie

Izzie had been uneasy about introducing Patricia to Jasper, and she'd been right. They certainly didn't hit it off right away. Of course, Jasper wanted things to go back to the way they used to be before Izzie had left. He was always coming over to see if she wanted to go swimming or jigging for mackerel, and when Patricia was included, he scowled. And Patricia couldn't understand why Izzie would want to have a boy for a best friend. "When I lived in England," she was fond of reminding Izzie, "I went to a private *girls'* school. No boys allowed."

When Izzie got a chance, she asked Jasper what he thought of Patricia.

"She's kinda stuck up, don't you think?" he said. "She hasn't got much to say about Granite

Cove that's even halfways nice."

"Well," said Izzie, "you got to remember it's all new to her. Besides, I have a feeling that she's more scared than snobby. But I'm not quite sure what she's got to be scared about. There's some hidden thing about her that I can't seem to figure out."

CHAPTER N_o 8

Later on, when Izzie thought back to their first two weeks in Granite Cove, she knew that it had all been just too good to be true. Or too good to last.

Everyone seemed to like Rosalie, and the women didn't even seem to mind when she caught on to the South Shore polka so fast at the first dance that all the men wanted to dance with her. The dance was held every two weeks in an old barn on the Morashes' property, with the music coming from Joe Murphy's fiddle and Mrs. Publicover's guitar. Rosalie loved the jumpy tunes and danced every single dance. But the women knew she'd be back in Woodside in six more weeks, so they just smiled and let it all happen.

Patricia took over feeding the chickens, and she looked so proud when she brought in the eggs that you'd have thought she'd laid them herself. She didn't make a fuss about all the fish they were eating, but she didn't say she liked it, either. A couple of times, they saw fires—or maybe explosions—out on the horizon, but Patricia didn't say that in England the fires and explosions were bigger. And she wasn't frowning at Jasper quite as much.

Mrs. Publicover practised away at her typewriter, and at last, she was using every one of her fingers. One day she said to Izzie, "Sometimes I love this machine so much that I almost want to hug it." Izzie laughed, and thought about what it would feel like to have all those hard metal keys digging into your chest. Mrs. Publicover did her typing practice in their little shop, and whenever her friends came in to buy thread or flour or salt, they made a big fuss about how clever she was. It was like getting a big bouquet of roses every day of her life.

And then the phone call came, right after supper on July 15. They'd had fish cakes for their meal. Izzie would always remember that, and it would be a long time before she'd allow herself to like fish cakes again.

Izzie answered the phone. The voice on the other end of the line said, "We need to verify your address. We have a telegram for Mrs. Bessie Publicover, and we have to know exactly where to bring it."

Izzie felt as though her heart had frozen inside her ribs. She knew that during a war, telegrams almost always mean bad news. No one sends a telegram to say that the sun is shining or that a parade is coming to town.

Izzie handed the phone to her mother. She watched her mother's face grow pale as she clutched the table for support. She gave the address to the caller, hung up the receiver, and sat down on the nearest chair.

"Now," said Mrs. Publicover in a hoarse voice, "is our time for waiting. We can't do anything but wait. We won't know anything until tomorrow."

At nine o'clock, they all went to bed, although it wasn't even dark yet. Izzie went in and climbed into her mother's big bed and hugged her for a while. But nobody did much sleeping that night.

It was a longer wait than they'd expected. They'd thought the telegram man would arrive right after breakfast on the following day—or maybe even earlier. But he didn't come until almost one o'clock. While they were waiting, everyone tried to keep busy. Mrs. Publicover went to practise on her typewriter, but when Izzie passed the door into their shop, she noticed that her mother's fingers were just lying on the keys, not moving. Many people came into the store to buy things and to be extra friendly. One or two people in the Cove had overheard the call on the phone's party line the evening before, so the news had spread like a flash fire. But no one admitted that they knew about it.

Izzie and Jasper and Patricia tried jigging for perch from Mr. Knickle's boat. They could see the road from there and would know when the telegram car arrived. But none of them cared whether or not they caught anything. Izzie felt mad at everybody. She got angry at Jasper when he lost one of the worms overboard. She snapped at Patricia when she said something perfectly innocent about English fish and chips. Later on, at noon, when they all went home for a dinner they couldn't eat, she actually told Joey to *shut up* when he came bouncing into the house with news about his morning. Then he started to cry, and this time it was herself that Izzie felt mad at.

After Rosalie had taken all their uneaten dinners and thrown them off the wharf for the gulls, they all continued to sit at the table, just staring at one another.

Mrs. Publicover shook her head. "I didn't know that waiting could ever be this hard or this long," she said.

That's when they heard the knock on their front door. No one ever used that door, so for a moment no one moved. Except, of course, Rosalie. She opened the door, and the telegram man stepped inside.

"A telegram for Mrs. Publicover," he said.

Izzie's mother stood up and took it from him without a word being spoken.

"A telegram for
Mrs. Publicover," he said.

With trembling hands, Mrs. Publicover opened the telegram. To Izzie it felt as though her mother were taking forever to read it. But she finally folded the telegram very slowly and carefully and put it back in the envelope. Then she took a deep breath, looked at all of them, and spoke.

"His ship was torpedoed," she said. There was quite a long pause before she went on. "It sank. They're now searching for survivors. In the meantime, your father is listed as 'missing.'" She sat down, clutching the telegram in her lap. "I'm too numb to cry," she said, "but if anyone else wants to do it, go right ahead."

Just then, Jasper opened the door, came in, and sat down on the couch beside Adella. He'd seen the telegram car arriving. When he heard what had happened, he said, "Listen. He's probably fine. A little wet and maybe cold, but fine. Remember last December when those three men came ashore in that lifeboat? Even though there'd been a big storm and tons of snow, they were a hundred percent OK."

Remembering the sight of those exhausted men in their lifeboat just made Izzie feel worse. "Oh, be quiet, Jasper!" she said. "Your own dad is home, eating his dinner. My dad is maybe dead. You don't understand *anything!*" Then she started to cry. She cried and cried, and felt as though she'd never stop. Even with Rosalie and her mother both hugging her, the crying went on and on. Finally, she managed to say, "I'm going up to Blueberry Hill. Nobody follow me. I want to be alone." She picked up her writing pad from a table by the porch and started out the door.

Patricia stood up, and just as Izzie stepped down to the driveway, Patricia said, "I envy you, Izzie." Then she looked very startled by what she'd just said.

Izzie stopped crying, stared at her, and hissed, "How can you *say* that, you stupid English snob?" Then she screamed at her, "I hate you! Go home to your own country and your dumb commander father, and leave us alone!" Then Izzie was gone, out through the path in the woods, headed for Blueberry Hill.

Up on the hill, she found her favourite flat rock and sat down. Then she took out her pad and wrote a letter to her father.

Dear Dad,

I'm scared that you're dead, but I'm trying hard not to believe it. Here are some things I want to say to you.

I'm sorry I got so mad at you when you came home and told us you'd joined the navy.

I'm sorry about the time I dropped your best penknife into the middle of the bay. I didn't mean to. It just slipped out of my hand.

Thank you for reading me stories before I went to bed.

Thank you for giving me Adella for my birthday when she was a little kitten.

Thank you for making me milk Clementine every morning. That's how I got to love her so much.

If you're in a lifeboat, keep rowing.

Please promise me you won't die.

XXOO Izzie

After a while, Izzie stood up and set out for home. She'd stopped crying but she felt numb and empty. As she was going down the hill, Izzie met Patricia climbing up. Her face was wet and her eyes were troubled.

"I know you said not to follow you," she said, "and your mother tried to prevent me from coming. But I had to disobey both of you."

Izzie stopped walking and just looked at Patricia. She didn't speak.

"Izzie," pleaded Patricia. "Try to forgive me for what I said. It was as though someone else were saying those words. I had no idea I was going to do it. I don't know why I did." Then she stopped talking for a moment. "Yes," she said, "I do know why. But I can't tell you. Maybe sometime, but not now. Maybe when we're both old ladies and aren't afraid of anything any more. I'm sorry, Izzie. I didn't mean to say that appalling thing."

Suddenly, Izzie felt too tired to stand up. They both sat down on a big fallen tree and were quiet for a few minutes. Then Izzie touched Patricia lightly on her shoulder and said, "It's OK, Patricia. I believe you. And I said some pretty terrible things myself. I don't hate you. I just don't *understand* you. You're so sort of ... *weird,* sometimes. Your commander father isn't dumb, and he's probably in as much danger as mine is ... or *was.*"

Izzie could feel the tears starting again. So she stood up, coughed a couple of times, and said, "Let's go home. We should maybe eat something. Rosalie gave our dinner to the gulls, and that was a while back." She checked her watch. "It's four o'clock."

When they reached the house, they could see that the kitchen was full of people. It hadn't taken the women of Granite Cove long. There was a big bowl of potato salad on the table, a plate of smoked salmon, a pan of hot sauerkraut, a casserole of macaroni and cheese, and three huge plates of cookies and doughnuts—the result of more ration stamps than Izzie could count.

Patricia looked puzzled. "Do the ladies around here always do this when there's trouble?"

"Yes," said Izzie, reaching for a molasses cookie. "They always do."

CHAPTER N.º 10

The Publicovers had found it agonizing to wait for the telegram that had brought the terrible news. During the next four days, they were to experience a different kind of waiting. Later in life, Izzie would say to her own children, "I don't know how we all survived during that time. It was a special kind of torture."

They each managed their fears in different ways. Joey, being so young, was the one with the shortest memory. He got together with his old friends and played as hard as he could play. Looking at him, you mightn't guess what was going on behind his smiling face. But he kept his eye on the road, watching for another telegram or letter to arrive.

Mrs. Publicover poured her misery into her typewriter. If her husband wasn't going to come back from the war, she'd be the one who'd have to support the family. She'd better learn how to do something that would bring in enough money to feed and clothe them. And she'd better learn how to do it *fast*.

Rosalie, of course, kept them all from falling apart at the seams. She was sympathetic when anyone seemed to need support, but at all times, her big smile was ready to warm them up. She cooked their favourite dishes—even salt herring and boiled potatoes, which she secretly hated— and looked after the customers in the shop when Mrs. Publicover was deep into her typing.

Patricia was the big surprise for all of them. She didn't *say* very much, but she *did* a lot of things. She took milking lessons from Izzie, and she learned how to clean out the stalls and bring fresh hay down from the loft. One day she wet-mopped the whole kitchen floor when it didn't really need it. She cleaned the lamp chimneys till they shone, and hummed "The White Cliffs of Dover" while she was doing it. And one day she went down to the Government Wharf, bought some cod tongues and cheeks from Mr. Henkel, brought them home, fried them up, and then pretended to enjoy eating them. She and Rosalie were almost like a mother and daughter as they planned the meals and kept the place running smoothly.

Izzie went around in a kind of fog. She'd stopped her wild crying, but she felt like the old family truck when it was shoved into neutral. It would kick over and jiggle a bit as long as the motor was on, but it wouldn't be going anywhere.

So Izzie spent some time with Jasper on the beach, just walking up and down and kicking the seaweed around. She forgot to milk Clementine twice, but Patricia did it, and never even mentioned having done so. One day Izzie found Patricia in the barn, talking to Clementine and crying. She didn't stop to listen to what Patricia was saying. She wanted to, but she figured it must be pretty private if the one Patricia was telling it to was a cow.

One morning, Izzie came into the kitchen in her stocking feet. Rosalie and her mother were over by the window, speaking in very low voices. They didn't hear her enter the room. Mrs. Publicover was saying, "All I can think about is him floating around in that water, trying to hang onto a piece of the broken ship. And maybe it's too cold for him to be able to do it. And—" here Mrs. Publicover gave two little sobs and then finished her sentence— "then maybe slipping under." Izzie squeezed her eyes shut and counted the days since the telegram had come. Three. Too many.

She tiptoed from the room and went out to the barn to sit on the milking stool beside Clementine. She laid her cheek against the cow's warm side and listened to her heart beating. "A beating heart means *life*," said Izzie, right out loud. "Thanks, Clementine," she whispered, "for trying to make me feel better."

That evening, after writing a letter to her father, Izzie said to Patricia, "Don't you want to write your mum and dad? I've got lots of paper—with lines. And we can get stamps from the mailman. Would you like to do that?"

"No," said Patricia.

"Why?" Izzie was puzzled. "It would make them feel good."

Patricia said something that sounded like "Humph." And then, "You haven't noticed any cartloads of mail arriving for *me,* have you? I don't *care* if they feel good."

"But your mum must be so lonesome for you. And—"

But Patricia interrupted Izzie. "Don't you worry," she said, "about my mother feeling lonesome for me. You never saw anyone as glad as she was to deposit me on a boat. All she ever cared about was how well I behaved myself. She jolly well acted as though she were the king's sister."

"But your dad? The … commander? Wouldn't he like a letter?"

Patricia's eyes filled with tears. Izzie could hardly hear her reply. "I don't think so," she said.

In the late afternoon of day five, Izzie and Patricia were looking out their bedroom window when they saw an official-looking car drive up to the Publicover house. For the second time, Izzie felt her heart freeze within her chest. Five days was too long to hang onto a piece of ship in the freezing cold Atlantic. Five days was too long for that car to be bringing good news. And Izzie knew that she wasn't ready to hear anything else.

Patricia grabbed Izzie's arm and squeezed it tight as they watched Mrs. Publicover go out to the car. A man in a uniform stepped out and handed her an envelope. Then the car drove away.

Suddenly, from downstairs, they could hear the sound of wild crying. Izzie had become used to seeing her mother cry, ever since Mr. Publicover had enlisted in the navy. But she'd never heard sounds like these. Very slowly, Izzie moved toward the stairs, with Patricia following behind her.

In the kitchen, they could see Mrs. Publicover with her face buried in her apron, and Rosalie holding her with both arms. Beside them on the table was the open message, and nearby, Joey stood, with his fist up to his mouth.

Izzie crossed the kitchen and stood in front of her mother.

"Mum," she said. *"Tell us."*

Mrs. Publicover took her apron away from her face and looked at all of them—her face wet, her nose and eyes a deep red. But she was able to speak—in a creaky kind of voice.

"He's fine," she said. "He's all right." Then she corrected herself. "Well," she said, "he's not exactly fine. And he's certainly not *all right*. He's probably very, *very* sick. But he's not *dead*. He's not at the bottom of the sea."

Then she read from the paper she'd left on the table. "Able Seaman Jeffrey Publicover has been rescued from a lifeboat in the mid–Atlantic. He is suffering from exposure, malnutrition, dehydration, and a severe case of hypothermia. He will be spending some time in the naval hospital in London before returning to his home for a month's sick leave."

Then, everyone was crying. Even Patricia. In fact, after everyone else had stopped, it seemed as though Patricia would go on forever. Both Mrs. Publicover and Rosalie were hugging her— one on each side.

When she finally stopped crying, Izzie looked around at all of them. Unlike Mrs. Publicover, whose nose and eyes were still shiny and red, Patricia's looked wet but almost normal. However, there was something new in her face that Izzie found hard to recognize or explain.

"Oh, my heavens!" said Patricia. "That was a lot of crying. But I was so afraid he'd drowned. I felt almost *certain* that he'd drowned. I'm sorry I once called him a sailor-boy. I did it to make you mad. And I guess I thought it might make me really believe that my father—Daddy—was a … commander."

There was a very long silence. No one knew what to say.

Finally Izzie spoke. "He isn't? What is he, then?"

Then Patricia started a storm of crying, all over again.

Izzie put her arm around her shoulder. "Never mind," she said. "You don't have to talk about it." But she was dying to know.

In the meantime, Rosalie and Mrs. Publicover kept very still, wanting Patricia to feel free to say whatever she might need to speak about.

"It's all right," said Patricia. "Or as you'd say, 'It's OK.'" Then she said, very slowly, "I think I want to tell you."

Everyone waited. Rosalie, usually so lively, stood as still as a rock. Mrs. Publicover slowly lowered herself into a chair. She'd had enough shocks for one day. They could hear the clock ticking, the gulls squawking, and a dog barking from way down by the beach. But nothing else.

Patricia cleared her throat and then looked straight at Izzie.

"He's what you Canadians would call a jailbird."

Izzie hoped that Patricia hadn't heard her gasp. But probably not. Patricia was still talking.

"He's been in the penitentiary ever since I was five. He stole some money. A *whole lot* of money. But I guess he wasn't a very successful criminal, because he was caught the very next day."

CHAPTER 12

It took a few moments for anyone to know how to respond. Izzie was the first to speak. "But why would your dad steal a pile of money?" she said. "I thought your folks were real fancy people." She knew she shouldn't say that, but it just came right out, before she could stop it.

"My mother *is*," said Patricia, blowing her nose on Rosalie's pink handkerchief. "Disgustingly fancy. Her mother—Granny—was an earl's daughter. Granny was always saying that Mummy had married beneath her, because Daddy was just a janitor in a building full of law offices. She'd even say those things when Daddy was in the same room. Even though I was only five, I can remember all that."

"Gee whiz!" exclaimed Izzie. "No one here would make a fuss because your father was a janitor. It's a *good* thing to be."

"Huh!" snorted Patricia. "Tell that to my *mother!*"

"If she felt like that … then, why …?"

"Ah, yes," sighed Patricia, rolling her eyes. "I'll tell you why. She was overcome by his ravishing male beauty and his bewitching charm. I remember *that,* too." She smiled a sad little smile.

"So she married him," said Izzie. "As a matter of fact, I think that's pretty romantic."

"No," stated Patricia. "It was *not* romantic. She married him because she was pregnant. An earl's granddaughter doesn't have a baby unless she's married. Nor does anyone else, for that matter. Not then, anyway. Not in those days. So, he married her."

Izzie couldn't help asking, "Did he love her?"

"Yes, he did. She was—*is*—very beautiful, and she was full of ginger when she was young and did a lot of wild and reckless things. I keep my ears open. I've heard her friends—even *Granny*—talking about what she used to be like."

There was a long pause. Izzie was trying to match up what she was hearing with the woman who wouldn't let her daughter cry.

After a brief silence, Patricia continued her story.

"Maybe she loved him for a while. I don't know. But it's not hard for me to recall everyone telling her that he was 'no good.' That's the term they used. That he wasn't good enough for her. That he didn't *measure up*. Did they think he didn't hear those things? They didn't like the way he *spoke* or his unruly hair or his table manners. I loved him a lot. I was only five, but I remember how kind he was to me. He'd put me on his shoulders and gallop around, pretending to be a horse. Or just hold me on his lap and listen to me talk."

Izzie was still puzzled. "But when he stole all that money …" She frowned. "Why did he need to do that? He had a perfectly good job. And why did people care about the way he spoke?"

Patricia looked at Izzie. "Remember the way the kids in school made fun of the way you and I talked when we first went to the Woodside school? Before the teacher made them stop? How would you like to hear that, day after day— and in your *very own home?*"

Patricia went on. It was as though she couldn't stop. "I think he took that money just so he could buy Mummy some big important thing, so that she'd understand how much he loved her, and so that she wouldn't feel he was so lower class and *no good*. Maybe a big expensive car like Granny's Rolls Royce, or a giant of a diamond ring with a necklace to match."

Izzie interrupted. "Who did he take the money from? And how come he got caught?" She thought she'd die if she couldn't know everything. She also found that there was a part of her that almost wished he'd gotten away with it and had been able to buy his beautiful wife a great big diamond ring to impress her snobby family. But she tried to push that thought out of her head.

"It's a long story," said Patricia, "but I'll tell you. He often had to do things at night—cleaning the places where the lawyers worked. They were very rich and had huge offices, with furniture to be polished and carpets to be cleaned. One evening he discovered that the door to one of the safes was open—just a little bit. He was probably dusting it or something. He opened it wider and saw an enormous bundle of hundred-pound notes. In those days, a pound was almost the same as five dollars. He could have bought a house with what was in that bundle of notes. Or two houses."

Patricia sighed. "So he took it. He hid the money in his equipment cart—in with the brushes and dusters and furniture polish—and closed the safe." She sighed again. "He'd never been a thief before, so he wasn't very good at it. He left his fingerprints all over the safe and its handle."

"But how did you know all that?" said Izzie. "You were only five years old."

Patricia wrinkled her brow. "My mother told me all those things when I was about eight, hoping it would make me stop missing him. Hoping it would make me hate him."

"And?" Izzie thought she knew the answer.

"It didn't work," said Patricia.

Rosalie came over and hugged Patricia, and Patricia hugged her back. But she kept on talking, right through the hug.

"I think Mummy was probably glad when he was caught. It left her free to entertain all her high-tone, classy, upper-crust boyfriends who were always out in our garden, pretending that they loved flowers—or taking her out on their big yachts or playing tennis with her. When the war came, they were all high-ranking commissioned officers, so they were even more exciting to her in their uniforms, with all those brass buttons and gold braid."

Patricia stared off into space for a while, looking out the window at the blue sea and the wheeling gulls, but not really seeing them.

"Did your dad ever write to you or anything? Did you and your mum ever go to visit him?" Izzie knew she sounded nosy, but that's what she was feeling. Besides, she thought she might burst wide open if she didn't know all the answers. This was the secret she'd been waiting for, and she didn't want to miss a single piece of it.

"No. When he was taken into custody—my mother refused to use the term *arrested*—it was as though he had disappeared into the bottom of a large, deep hole. No one talked about him—ever. If I said I missed him or cried about him being gone, I was sent to my room. I was told not to mention him or think about him. Not mentioning him was hard, but I managed it. But they couldn't do anything about my thoughts."

Patricia took a deep breath. "I think it was around that time that Mummy decided that if she couldn't have a perfect husband, she was going to have a perfect child. That's when she became so stiff and proper and sort of … *frozen.* That's why I was never allowed to cry or behave angrily, or have problems or act unhappy. But no matter how hard I tried, I just seemed to be in everyone's way—my mother's, the boyfriends', and even Granny's. I think I just reminded them of Daddy. And …" She paused.

"And?" Izzie prompted her.

"And when Mummy heard that the government was shipping children overseas to Canada to keep them safe from the bombs, she could hardly wait to start packing my valises."

"Valises?"

"Suitcases. Bags. Luggage."

Patricia looked around the kitchen and grinned a lopsided smile at them all. *"There!"* she said, slapping her knees with her hands. "Now you know my whole life story." Then she added,

"It makes me feel kind of weak in the knees to tell it; but it feels good, too, to get it all out."

"And it's time we all had supper," said Mrs. Publicover, as she moved toward the stove, giving Patricia a little squeeze on the arm as she went by. "And I'd better rescue those baked potatoes before they shrivel up like prunes."

CHAPTER No 13

The next day was one of those perfect Nova Scotia days that the tourist brochures talk about. The air was clear and warm—but not hot—and the gulls were a blinding white against the blue sky, sailing along on the air currents, scarcely moving. The boats were chugging in from their morning's work, and they shone vividly in the bright sunshine—blue, orange, yellow, red.

Jasper and Patricia and Izzie went for a swim on the beach, jigged for mackerel from Mr. Henkel's flat, and stuffed themselves with Indian pears over by Swallow Lake. No one seemed to be jealous of anybody any more. There'd been so many shocks and fears and shared drama that the three kids had come to accept one another. They were more like a set of triplets.

On the way home, Patricia said, "I love this place. I love your family and Rosalie. I love Clementine. I even love the oil lamps. And of course I love listening in on the party line telephone. I try not to think about going home when the war's over."

Then Izzie spoke. "I've been thinking, Patricia ..."

"Yes? What have you been thinking?"

"That it might be a really nice idea—for him—*and* for you—if you wrote your dad a letter."

"He's never written *me* one. Not once."

"But when he left, you were too young to be able to read. And he probably thought it would make your mother mad."

"I don't know, Izzie," said Patricia. She was frowning and running her hand up and down a stick she was carrying. "I'd feel as though I were writing to a stranger."

"You *would* be writing to a stranger. But even ordinary pen pals get to know each other pretty fast."

Patricia raised her eyebrows. "That's right," she said. "I once had a pen pal in Australia, when I was about nine years old. After a few letters, I felt that she was like my own sister."

They walked along in silence for a while. Then, as they turned up the path to the Publicover house, Patricia stopped and looked at Izzie.

"I'll do it!" She almost yelled it. "What time does the postman pick up the letters tomorrow?"

"At about eleven in the morning."

"There'll be one from me. To my father. I know where he is. I found the address one day when I was hunting for an old doll in a trunk in our attic. I wrote it down in a little book I have for writing down my thoughts. I must have known I was going to do this someday. I must have known I *wanted* to do it."

When Patricia turned to look at Izzie, both of them were grinning so hard that it was a wonder their faces didn't crack.

The rest of the summer passed without any family disasters, although everyone was very aware of the ongoing war. They still saw occasional airplanes on the horizon, and there was a rumour of fishermen in Halibut Cove actually seeing an enormous submarine sliding under their boat one day, when they were hauling in their mackerel nets. In that same village, Mr. Jackson's son Jamie came home with one blind eye, and over in Conrad's Harbour, the Jodreys' oldest boy arrived back from the war minus a leg. Somebody's uncle from Big Gull Harbour had even been killed during the Dieppe raid. There was a lot of uneasiness among families who had fathers or sons or daughters in the war.

But Mrs. Publicover was looking truly happy for the first time since her husband had joined the navy. "Ever since your father was found in that lifeboat," she said, "everything seems easy and simple for me—milking cows, doing laundry on a scrub board, carrying water, and especially learning to type." She grinned and gave the type-writer a little pat.

"And you're getting really *fast*," said Izzie.

"What's more," put in Patricia, "I noticed yesterday that you were doing it on all the keys. Jolly good, I'd say!"

"I *know!*" said Mrs. Publicover and then laughed. "I haven't felt this smart since I won a spelling prize in Grade One."

No one mentioned that no letter had come from England for Patricia. She watched the arrival of the mail truck each day, but she didn't rush out to check the box. And when someone else brought in the letters, she pretended she was doing something else and avoided looking at anybody.

"Maybe he was moved to another prison," suggested Izzie.

"Or," said Rosalie, "don't forget that his letter could have been on a ship that was torpedoed."

"It's OK," said Patricia, looking as though it was *not* OK. "Maybe I just wasn't meant to have a nice family. But at least I *tried*."

A week later, it was time to leave Granite Cove and return to Woodside. The Eisners were returning on the following morning, so Mrs. Publicover left a tuna casserole in the homemade icebox for them. They packed up all their belongings in the truck and said their goodbyes to everyone, including Clementine. But this time the Publicovers were less sad. They knew they would return—maybe even next summer—and Izzie's father would be coming home for a month's leave, sometime soon.

Jasper came over to say goodbye—this time bringing two boxes of notepaper. "Izzie can write to me on Sundays," he said, "and Patricia on Wednesdays. I want two letters a week. So don't let me down. I'll keep them so that both of you can read them in your old age."

This time it was Patricia's eyes that were leaking tears as the truck drove out of Granite Cove and around the bend that hid their view of the sea. As they moved on toward the road to Halifax, they could see the mail truck approaching.

"Let's make him stop," said Izzie. "I wrote a goodbye letter to Jasper last night, and this way he'll get it real fast."

When Mr. Robb, the mailman, saw their truck stop in the middle of the road, he put on his brakes and drew up beside them. Before Izzie could give her letter to him, he leaned out the window and said, "I've got an envelope here for Patricia Witherspoon, care of the Publicovers." He reached back to dig something out of his mailbag. Then his arm stretched out the window and handed a large brown envelope into the truck. In the top left corner was the name Julian Witherspoon and his address. Then the Publicover truck drove on.

Patricia hugged the brown envelope for a long time and made no move to open it. To Izzie, it seemed like a week.

"For Pete's sake, Patricia," she said. "*Open* it."

"Suppose it's horrible," said Patricia, hugging it harder. "Suppose he sounds like an awful person. Suppose he's *offended* because I wrote to him. Besides ..."

"Besides what? *What?*" Izzie felt as though she'd collapse in a heap if Patricia didn't hurry up and open that letter.

"Besides ... I think I want to be alone when I read it. I don't know why. I just do." Patricia sighed.

Izzie tried to get inside Patricia's head, to imagine what she was thinking and feeling. Finally she said, "Well, OK. I can see that this is a pretty ...," she searched for the right word, "*momentous* occasion. I can understand—or

This time it was Patricia's eyes that were leaking tears as the truck drove out of Granite Cove and around the bend that hid their view of the sea.

almost understand—that you might want to be alone to read it."

Izzie paused again. "But couldn't you maybe open the end of the envelope and take just a little *peek* inside? Probably his very first sentence will tell you if it's going to be good or bad. It takes almost two hours to get to Woodside, with the ferry and all. By the time we get there, you'll probably be dead from the suspense—unless you find out *something*."

Patricia stared at Izzie, eyes wide open, not blinking, but she was fingering the end of the envelope.

"Go *on*!" exclaimed Izzie. "*Do* it! It can't be any worse than what you've been thinking ever since you were *five. Open it!*"

Patricia started blinking again. "Maybe I will," she whispered. "I'll just take ever so tiny a peek."

Her hands were shaking as she carefully opened the end of the envelope. Then, biting her bottom lip, she widened it a bit and looked inside.

"There are pages and pages and pages!" she exclaimed. "That's why the envelope's so big." She gazed at Izzie with a look of astonishment.

Izzie could scarcely keep her hands off the envelope. "Well—what does he *say?* Like after 'Dear Patricia'?"

Patricia shuffled through the pages till she came to the first one. Her voice was trembling as she read. *"Dear Patricia, Getting your letter was the best thing that has happened to me in the past six years."*

Izzie let out a yelp of pleasure, and then noticed that Patricia was hugging the letter again and that tears were streaming down her face.

"You OK?"

"Yes," said Patricia, between gulps. "*Very* OK. I think I feel a lot the way you did when you learned that your father was alive, after he was missing for so long. It's a happy kind of crying."

Then Patricia added, "And now I can tell you why I said that I envied you on that awful day when you learned your father was missing. Inside, I knew that I'd rather have a father who was missing, but whom I'd known and loved, than have a father whom I didn't know and who was locked up somewhere in a terrible place. I didn't mean to *say* it, but I meant what I said."

Then Patricia laughed, really hard. "Wouldn't my mother be angry right now! Two bad things: I'm crying, and that would put her in a terrible fit. But worst of all, the jailbird and his daughter are now writing letters to each other. And both of them seem to be very pleased with the arrangement."

The truck jogged along in the direction of Halifax. Soon, they'd be crossing the harbour on the ferry and driving through Dartmouth and into Woodside. This time it would be another kind of homecoming. And a new chapter in their lives was about to open up for all of them.

Dear Reader,

Welcome back to Our Canadian Girl! In addition to this story about Izzie, there are many more adventures of other spirited girls to come.

So please keep on reading. And do stay in touch. You can also log on to our website at www.ourcanadiangirl.ca and enjoy fun activities, sample chapters, a fan club, and monthly contests.

Sincerely,
Barbara Berson
Editor

1608
Samuel de Champlain establishes the first fortified trading post at Quebec.

1759
The British defeat the French in the Battle of the Plains of Abraham.

1812
The United States declares war against Canada.

1845
The expedition of Sir John Franklin to the Arctic ends when the ship is frozen in the pack ice; the fate of its crew remains a mystery.

1869
Louis Riel leads his Métis followers in the Red River Rebellion.

1871
British Columbia joins Canada.

1755
The British expel the entire French population of Acadia (today's Maritime provinces), sending them into exile.

1776
The 13 Colonies revolt against Britain, and the Loyalists flee to Canada.

1837
Calling for responsible government, the Patriotes, following Louis-Joseph Papineau, rebel in Lower Canada; William Lyon Mackenzie leads the uprising in Upper Canada.

1867
New Brunswick, Nova Scotia and the United Province of Canada come together in Confederation to form the Dominion of Canada.

1870
Manitoba joins Canada. The Northwest Territories become an official territory of Canada.

1783
Rachel

1865
Angelique

Timeline

1885
At Craigellachie, British Columbia, the last spike is driven to complete the building of the Canadian Pacific Railway.

1898
The Yukon Territory becomes an official territory of Canada.

1914
Britain declares war on Germany, and Canada, because of its ties to Britain, is at war too.

1918
As a result of the Wartime Elections Act, the women of Canada are given the right to vote in federal elections.

1945
World War II ends conclusively with the dropping of atomic bombs on Hiroshima and Nagasaki.

1873
Prince Edward Island joins Canada.

1896
Gold is discovered on Bonanza Creek, a tributary of the Klondike River.

1905
Alberta and Saskatchewan join Canada.

1917
In the Halifax harbour, two ships collide, causing an explosion that leaves more than 1,600 dead and 9,000 injured.

1939
Canada declares war on Germany seven days after war is declared by Britain and France.

1949
Newfoundland, under the leadership of Joey Smallwood, joins Canada.

1942
Izzie

1944
Margit